Disney
Princess

Also From Joe Books

Disney Princess Comics Treasury

Disney Frozen Cinestory Comic

Disney Cinderella Cinestory Comic

Disney Alice in Wonderland Cinestory Comic

Disney Princess Comic Strips Collection Volume One

Disney Princess Comic Strips Collection Volume Two

Disney Tangled Cinestory Comic

Disney Tangled Before Ever After Cinestory Comic

Disney Beauty and the Beast Cinestory Comic

Disney Snow White and the Seven Dwarfs Cinestory Comic

Disney Snow White and the Seven Dwarfs Cinestory Comic Collector's Edition

Disney
Princess
Something to Sing About
ROCKFORD PUBLIC LIBRARY
JOE BOOKS LTD

Published simultaneously in the United States and Canada by Joe Books Ltd,
489 College Street, Suite 203, Toronto, ON M6G 1A5.

www.joebooks.com

First Joe Books edition: December 2017

Print ISBN: 978-1-77275-522-0

Library and Archives Canada Cataloguing in Publication
information is available upon request.

Printed and bound in Canada
1 3 5 7 9 10 8 6 4 2

Disney
Princess
Something to Sing About

Written by Paul Benjamin, Geoffrey Golden, Emma Hambly, Oliver Ho, Arie Kaplan, Megan Kearney, Charli McEachran, Deanna McFadden, Chris Meades, Tea Orsi, and Patrick Storck

Illustrated by Egle Bartolini, Dylan Bonner, Nicole Dalcin, Chris Dreier, Jason Flores-Holz, Brianna Garcia, Nolen Lee, Mitch Leeuwe, and Steph Lew

Colored by Dylan Bonner, Wes Dzioba, Matt Herms, Brianna Garcia, Paul Little, and Donovan Yuciuk

Cover by Dylan Bonner

Lettered by AndWorld Design and Nicole Dalcin

Series edited by Steffie Davis, Jennifer Hale, and Deanna McFadden

MUCH DISHWARE ABOUT NOTHING

YOUR BREAKFAST IS ON ITS WAY, HONEY!
MMM, IT'S GOING TO BE DELICIOUS!

ET VOILÃ!
WOW! MAYBE YOU OVERDID IT A BIT, DARLING?

NAH, YOU DESERVE THE BEST BEIGNETS IN ALL NEW ORLEANS!
AND THE SMALLEST, TOO!

TAKE YOUR TIME! I KNOW YOU LOVE RELAXING BREAKFASTS...

THAT WAS GREAT! BUT I'M STILL A LITTLE BIT HUNGRY...
GURGLE
PHEW! I'M SO GLAD YOU LIKED IT!

THE RECIPE WAS TRICKY, AND SOME OF THE BEIGNETS GOT BURNED, BUT...

...I LEARNED HOW TO USE SO MANY TOOLS, AND NOW I'M READY TO WORK IN THE KITCHEN WITH YOU!

SO...WILL YOU LET ME HELP YOU SOMETIMES?
HOW ABOUT STARTING WITH THE WASHING UP?
End

CRAZY RIDE

SHOO NOW, YE WEE HORSE LICE!

OKAY, IF YE WANT TO GO FOR A RIDE, WE'LL GO FOR A RIDE *TOGETHER!*

SWOOSH
HOLD ON TIGHT!

EVERYTHING OKAY BACK THERE, BOYS?!?

THAT WAS THE SOFTEST LANDING *EVER*, ANGUS!

SO...WHERE ARE WE GOIN' NEXT?
THUD

COME BACK! THE FUN HAS JUST BEGUN!

MAYBE THEY'LL STICK TO HORSEY RIDES WITH DAD FROM NOW ON!
End

BIRD'S EYE VIEW

THAT ONE LOOKS LIKE A RABBIT WITH THREE EARS... AND THAT ONE LOOKS LIKE AN UPSIDE-DOWN... QUESTION MARK... YAWN

THE LAST TIME THIS HAPPENED I WASTED MY CHANCE, BUT STAY... RIGHT... THERE.

JUST SIT STILL A LITTLE LONGER, PLEASE. I REALLY APPRECIATE THE BIRD'S-EYE VIEW!
End

STAGE STRUCK

I'VE WRITTEN A PLAY FOR YOU AND ALL OF THE OTHER ***ENCHANTED OBJECTS*** TO PERFORM, BUT I WASN'T SURE IF ANY OF THEM WERE INTERESTED IN ACTING IN IT--

WHOOSH

ER...I ***THINK*** IT'S SAFE TO SAY THEY'RE ***INTERESTED.***

YOU KNOW, I'D BE ***HAPPY*** TO SUPPLY ALL OF THE ***COSTUMES*** FOR THE PLAY.
WELL, MOST OF THE ENCHANTED OBJECTS ARE ***TOO SMALL*** TO WEAR COSTUMES.

I'M SURE I CAN FIND ***SOMETHING*** FOR THEM TO WEAR.
HOW ABOUT THIS ONE?
NOPE, SORRY.

MOMENTS LATER...
HOW ABOUT THIS ONE?
NOPE!

LATER STILL...
THIS ONE?
NOPE.
SIGH...

OKAY EVERYONE, FROM THE TOP!
WAIT...

WE CAN'T BEGIN REHEARSAL YET.
WHY NOT?

ER...IT'S LUMIERE.
IS HE SICK?
NOT "SICK," SO MUCH AS "IN LOVE"...

...WITH **HIMSELF.**
WHO IS THE MOST **HANDSOME** CANDELABRA **IN THE ENTIRE WORLD?**

BE OUR GUEST, BE OUR GUEST...

PUT OUR SERVICE TO THE TEST...
UM...LUMIERE...

WHAT'S WRONG, BELLE? AREN'T I GIVING A GOOD PERFORMANCE?
OH YOU DEFINITELY **ARE,** IT'S JUST THAT...

...YOU'RE NOT PERFORMING **MY PLAY.**
OOPS.

AH, THE SCARLET CANDELABRA! GOOD TO SEE YOU!
YES, 'TIS I!!

GOOD JOB EVERYONE, BUT JUST BE CAREFUL.
"CAREFUL" ABOUT WHAT?
YOU DON'T WANT TO BE TOO LOUD!
OH COME ON, WHO WOULD NOT LOVE TO HEAR...

...THE DULCET TONES OF MY BOOMING VOICE??
GRRRRR...

WHAT'S WRONG?
YOU'RE ALL DOING A WONDERFUL JOB WITH YOUR PLAY, BUT I WAS WONDERING IF YOU COULD REHEARSE JUST A LITTLE BIT MORE...QUIETLY.

QUIETLY? QUIETLY?? WE'RE TOO LOUD? THIS IS OUTRAGEOUS, AND I FOR ONE WILL NOT STAND HERE--

GRRRRR....

YOU KNOW, NOW THAT I THINK OF IT, WE WERE BEING TOO LOUD!

SCARLET CANDELABRA! WILL YOU SAVE US FROM THE DUKE'S EVIL HENCHMEN?
BUT OF COURSE! BECAUSE I AM--

...THE SCARLET CANDELABRA!!
COME ON! NOW THEY'RE WHISPERING LOUDLY!

ISN'T THERE A TYPE OF ACTING THAT YOU HAVE TO DO QUIETLY?
PANTOMIME

HMM...
PANTOMIME

IT WAS SUCH A GOOD IDEA TO REWRITE THE PLAY AS A PANTOMIME SHOW! STILL, IT DOES SEEM LIKE IT'S MISSING SOMETHING...

WASN'T MY PERFORMANCE AMAZING??
THERE IT IS!
End

SHARK DREAMS

THERE'S NOTHING AS RELAXING AS A NICE AFTERNOON SWIM.

I COULDN'T AGREE MORE!

OH, DON'T WORRY. I'M TOO TIRED TO BE DANGEROUS.

I HAVEN'T SLEPT IN...EVER!

YOU'VE NEVER SLEPT? WHEN DO YOU DREAM?

I GUESS I DREAM ALL THE TIME.

WHAT DO YOU DREAM OF?

MOSTLY THE WORLD ABOVE SEA.
ME TOO!!!

I LOVE THE AIR FISH.
THOSE ARE CALLED "BIRDS"!

I EVEN KNOW ONE NAMED SCUTTLE. HE'S THE BEST!
YOU KNOW AN AIR FISH? DOES HE SING?

ACTUALLY, I SING, BUT HE--
SONGS ABOUT HOW WHALES ARE ALWAYS PLOTTING AGAINST US.

I THINK NOT SLEEPING HAS MADE YOU A LITTLE PARANOID.
I WOULDN'T RULE IT OUT.

DO YOU EVER CHASE THE FLOATING ISLANDS?
I DON'T THINK I'VE EVER SEEN ONE.

THEY'RE BIG AND AND HAVE BOOMING TUBES AND LITTLE CREATURES AND FLAGS.
OH, I THINK YOU MEAN "SHIPS".

I MAKE FRIENDS WITH THEM PRETTY EASILY. I THINK BECAUSE OF MY SMILE.
REALLY?

OH, SURE. WHEN THEY SEE ME, THEY YELL ***"CHUM!"*** AND THROW ME SOME LUNCH!

DO YOU EVER WANT TO SWIM UP WHEN IT'S DARK TO THOSE LANTERN FISH THEY HAVE?
WELL AT NIGHT, I'M USUALLY -- OH, RIGHT. SORRY.

I'VE NEVER SEEN ANY LANTERN FISH, THOUGH.
THEY'RE WAY DEEP UP THERE, LIKE OURS ARE WAY DOWN DEEP HERE.

EVERY NIGHT THEY LINE UP THE SAME WAY AND MOVE ACROSS THE SKY. THEY FORM SHAPES AND PICTURES, AND SOME OF THEM JUST ZIP ALONG REALLY FAST.

I THINK THOSE ARE CALLED "STARS".
I'VE SEEN STAR FISH. THEY DON'T TWINKLE.

WELL, I SHOULD GET GOING. I NEED TO REST A LITTLE. IT'S BEEN A PLEASURE!

I THOUGHT YOU SAID YOU COULDN'T SLEEP.

NO, BUT SOMETIMES I LET THE CURRENTS THAT RUN ALONG THE LAND DO MOST OF THE SWIMMING FOR ME.

THAT'S WHY THEY CALL IT THE ***COAST!***
End

CHECKERS

OKAY, SO THOSE ARE THE BASIC RULES. YOU'RE SURE YOU HAVE NEVER PLAYED BEFORE?

WHAT ARE YOU TWO UP TO?
I'M TEACHING ABU TO PLAY CHECKERS.

YOU'RE TEACHING *HIM?* AH, OKAY.

I HAVE A FEELING HE'LL BE A FAST LEARNER. I WOULDN'T PUT ANY MONEY ON IT, THOUGH.

REMEMBER, YOU CAN ONLY MOVE ONE SPACE DIAGONALLY. NOW YOU GO.

NO! IT HAS TO STAY ON THE TABLE!

NO, JUST LEAVE IT TO THE SIDE. WE'LL CHALK IT UP TO "BEGINNER'S YUCK."

THIS IS CALLED A "JUMP." IF YOU CAN GO OVER AN OPPONENT'S PIECE TO AN EMPTY SPACE, YOU CAN LAND ON THAT EXTRA SPACE...

...AND THEN YOU CAN TAKE THEIR PIECE OFF THE BOARD!

LET ME CLARIFY...

EEP!!!
WHAT IS IT?

CLUNK
AH, I SEE. IT WAS A DISTRACTION.

YOU AREN'T ALLOWED TO TAKE PIECES. THAT'S CHEATING! NOW PICK IT UP.

EVERYTHING YOU ARE DOING NOW IS ALSO CHEATING. EVERYTHING.

YOU LEFT A CORNER OPEN, SO THIS PIECE IS MINE. YOUR MOVE.

THAT'S DEFINITELY A MOVE I'VE NEVER SEEN BEFORE.

SO HOW ARE THE LESSONS COMING ALONG?

?
WELL, HE PULLED THE BAGHDAD BEETLE FLIP, THE SAND SWITCHEROO, A MIDNIGHT DOUBLE CLOUD, AND A NEW VARIATION ON THE SCARAB SHUFFLE.

OH, YOU THOUGHT I WAS FALLING FOR THOSE ***EASY*** SCAMS? I WAS LEARNING YOUR OTHER TRICKS. AND YOUR SLEIGHT OF HAND IS GETTING A LITTLE LAZY, LATELY.

SHE LIKES TO KEEP HER STRATEGY ONE JUMP AHEAD, TOO.
End

RAPUNZEL

OH MY GOSH, PASCAL, I HAD NO IDEA YOU COULD EAT AN ENTIRE BOWL OF STRAWBERRIES IN ONE SITTING.

THEY REALLY ARE HAIR TODAY, GONE TOMORROW!

WHAT WAS THAT? MY JOKES ARE HAIRRIBBLE? I'M SORRY, I CAN'T HAIR YOU!

WHAT DO YOU EXPECT PASCAL? MY NAME IS RAPUNZEL!
End

NOT A WORRY

MEEKO, WHAT'S WRONG?

ARE YOU SICK?
PSHAW, THAT RACCOON ISN'T SICK, CHILD, HE'S JUST...

BWOOORP

...'DIGESTING'
End

SURPRISE

BOYS, YOU'VE BEEN SLACKING OFF DURING COMBAT TRAINING.

WHAT COULD BE MORE IMPORTANT?

CREATING THE PERFECT FIREWORKS DISPLAY.

WHY DIDN'T YOU SAY SO?

HERE'S THE FIREWORKS ROCKET I CREATED. I'VE DESIGNED IT TO SHOOT OUT BRIGHT WHITE SPARKS WHEN IT EXPLODES IN THE SKY.

THIS IS MINE. IT DISPLAYS MULTI-COLORED STARS. THAT IS, IT WILL IF IT WORKS THE WAY IT'S SUPPOSED TO.

THIS ROCKET IS CALLED "FEARLESS LEADER," AND OBVIOUSLY, I NAMED IT AFTER MYSELF.

MY ROCKET IS NAMED "YAO," BECAUSE LIKE HIM, IT'S SHORT, STUBBY, AND FULL OF NOISE.
HEY!!

OKAY, WE'VE DESIGNED THE FIREWORKS. WE'VE DECORATED THEM. BUT I STILL FEEL LIKE I'M FORGETTING SOMETHING...

YAAAAAAAAA....

...AAAAAAAAAA!!

OH YEAH. I FORGOT THAT I WAS WORKING WITH THOSE THREE. WHICH MEANS THINGS LIKE THAT WILL HAPPEN.
NOT THAT I'D HAVE IT ANY OTHER WAY.

MUSHU, WHAT'S WRONG?
ARE YOU MAKING A FIREWORKS DISPLAY WITHOUT ME?

WELL YES, BUT WE HAD A GOOD REASON.
"A GOOD REASON"? SHE SAYS SHE HAS A GOOD REASON. WHAT COULD POSSIBLY BE A GOOD REASON FOR LEAVING ME OUT OF THE LOOP?

WELL, THAT IS JUST ABOUT THE MOST HANDSOME ROCKET I'VE EVER SEEN. BUT DON'T THINK IT GETS YOU OFF THE HOOK!

OKAY, SO FIRST YOU DECIDE TO PUT ON A FIREWORKS DISPLAY WITHOUT EVEN ASKING IF I WANT TO BE A PART OF IT.

AND **THEN** YOU HAVE THE AUDACITY -- THE **NERVE** -- TO MAKE ONE OF YOUR ROCKETS RESEMBLE ME. WHY?

BECAUSE WHEN WE LAUNCH IT, IT'LL RELEASE A TORRENT OF SPARKS THAT FORM...**YOU.** MUSHU THE DRAGON. IT'S A **MUSHU-SHAPED FIREWORKS DISPLAY.** IT WAS SUPPOSED TO BE A SURPRISE.

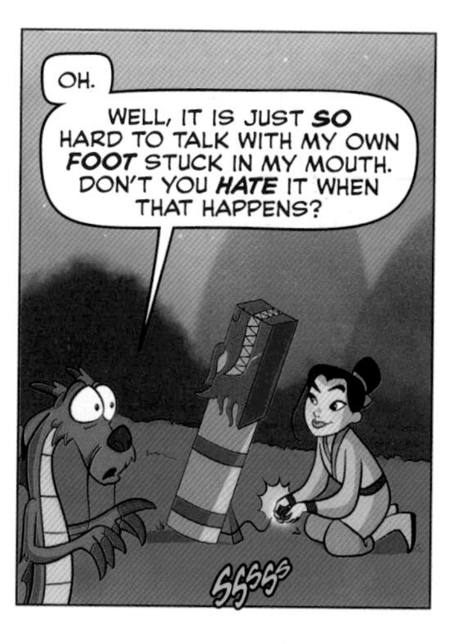
OH.
WELL, IT IS JUST **SO** HARD TO TALK WITH MY OWN **FOOT** STUCK IN MY MOUTH. DON'T YOU **HATE** IT WHEN THAT HAPPENS?
SSSSS

DON'T YOU UNDERSTAND? WE CREATED THE "MUSHU" ROCKET TO SHOW YOU HOW MUCH YOU MEAN TO ALL OF US.
SHOOOOOOM

WOW.

IF I'M BEING **HONEST,** THOUGH, YOU **DID** MAKE MY EYES TOO CLOSE TOGETHER.
KIDDING! JUST KIDDING!
End

SOMETHING COLD

IT'S TOO HOT TO MOVE.
I CAN DO SOMETHING ABOUT THAT!

UH-OH.
WE MIGHT END UP AT THE NORTH POLE!

WE'D BETTER STOP HIM BEFORE OUR KINGDOM TURNS TO ICE!

WHERE ARE *YOU* GOING?
End

HAIRMONY

OH!
SNAP

I THOUGHT I HAD A SPARE AROUND HERE... SOMEWHERE...

OKAY, PASCAL, LET'S TRY A LITTLE HAIR-MONY...
End

WINDY WOES

WHAT ARE YOU LOOKING AT?

?!
WHOOSH

!!!
WHOOSH

I ADMIRE HIS DETERMINATION.

FLIT HAS BEEN TRYING TO GET THAT FLOWER ALL DAY.

THE WIND KEEPS BLOWING IT AWAY.
HE CAN HELP HIMSELF TO THESE ONES HERE. THEY ARE OUT OF THE WIND.

I GUESS HE PREFERS FAST FOOD!

End

LAVA

YOU KNOW THE RULES PASCAL...

FIRST ONE TO TOUCH THE ***HOT LAVA*** LOSES!

I DON'T CONSIDER THIS CHEATING, DO YOU?

THREE DAYS LATER.
OBVIOUSLY, IT'S A TIE.
End

BASHFUL

IT'S RAINING SO HARD OUTSIDE!

THAT MAKES IT A PERFECT DAY TO DO THINGS INSIDE.

OH! HELLO!

IS SOMETHING WRONG?
WELL...

IT'S OKAY. YOU CAN TELL ME.
UM...

WHERE ARE YOU GOING?

CAN YOU HEAR ME IN THERE?

NOW YOU RELAX AND TELL ME WHAT IS WRONG.

DO YOU NEED SOME SPACE?

IS THIS BETTER? FURTHER?

I SAID, ***"IS THIS FAR ENOUGH?"***

I'M SORRY, BUT YOU'LL HAVE TO SPEAK UP. IT'S HARD TO HEAR YOU OVER THE RAIN.

THUMP

THUMP
AND THUNDER!

OH, BASHFUL! THAT GUITAR IS OFF KEY.

BAD KEY? IS THAT IT? YOU NEED A KEY?

IT'S A GOOD THING I KEEP A SPARE.
NOTHING LIKE WAITING IN THE RAIN AFTER A HARD DAY'S WORK.
End

HURRY BACK

I'M SO LATE FOR THE FESTIVAL!
NOT TO WORRY.

I TAUGHT MEEKO HOW TO BRAID QUICKLY.

THANK YOU! I MUST HURRY BA--

--ACK!
End

SAUCY INVENTION

PRESENTING MY LATEST INVENTION: AN AUTOMATED SAUCE BOAT! YOU SIMPLY PULL THE LEVER AND THIS CONTRAPTION DOES THE POURING FOR YOU.
HOW WONDERFUL!

THIS LEVER ALLOWS YOU TO ADJUST HOW MUCH SAUCE IS DISTRIBUTED PER POUR.
PAPA, THE DEVICE IS--

SPLAT

IT MIGHT NEED A *LITTLE* MORE WORK.
I AGREE, BELLE. THE SAUCE NEEDS MORE ONION.
End

EYES CLOSED

WHOOSH
ACK!

IT'S **OKAY!** I'M **FINE!**

I CAN SHOOT JUST AS WELL IN THE DARK.
End

DRY TIME

THWOSH

NOTHING LIKE A NICE, WINDY DAY OUTSIDE TO DRY MY HAIR A LITTLE FASTER.

???

!!!

?

NO, NO, NO, NO! **OW!**

I **SAID,** "CAN YOU PLEASE UNTIE MY HAIR WHILE YOU'RE OVER THERE?"

WHAT? FOOD? SURE, YOU CAN HAVE A TREAT AFTER YOU UNTIE MY HAIR!

NO! WHERE ARE YOU GOING? CUT IT OUT!

COME BACK HERE!!!

GREAT. NOW WHAT?

KRA-KOW

SPLAPP

SPLASH
SLUSH

I'M SORRY, BUT YOU ALREADY ATE EVERYTHING!

YOU HAD YOUR CHANCE. NOW YOU HAVE TO WAIT FOR THIS TO DRY TO GET BACK DOWN.

THEN I DISCARD?
CHT! CHT!
I'M SORRY, I ONLY EVER LEARNED SOLITAIRE.
End

A GIFT TO REMEMBER

SO...TELL ME AGAIN, DEAR, WHAT DOES THIS BOOK...DO?
THAT'S A NEVER-FORGET JOURNAL.

YOU CAN WRITE IN IT EVERYTHING YOU NEED TO REMEMBER...
OH! WHAT A BEAUTIFUL GIFT!

I'M AFRAID I MUST LEAVE NOW, DEAR! THOUGH... I CAN'T REMEMBER WHY...
SEE? WITH YOUR NEW JOURNAL, THIS WILL NEVER HAPPEN AGAIN!

AS LONG AS YOU REMEMBER TO TAKE IT, OF COURSE...
End

WORKOUT

AERIAL ACROBATICS

JUMP BRAID

MEDUSA SNAKE WAVES

ARM PULLS
End

QUEEN FOR A DAY

SINCE I'M **UNDER THE WEATHER,** JASMINE, YOU'LL HAVE TO **RULE IN MY PLACE...**
...FOR **TODAY,** ANYWAY!
O-OKAY, FATHER.

YOU'LL SIT ON THE THRONE AND ATTEND TO ALL MY BUSINESS MATTERS.
OF COURSE!

OH, AND ONE OTHER THING...
YES?

TELL **ABU** TO **GET OFF OF ME!**
HE'S **JUST** TRYING TO GIVE YOU A SOOTHING MASSAGE...

8:00AM
CONSIDER THIS ROYAL PROCLAMATION SIGNED!

8:30AM
AND CONSIDER **THIS OTHER** ROYAL PROCLAMATION SIGNED!

9:00AM
...AND CONSIDER **THIS** OTHER--
HEY, WHERE'D THE PROCLAMATION GO?

YOU'RE JUST AS BORED AS **I** AM, **AREN'T** YOU, RAJAH?

WAIT A MINUTE! I'M THE **QUEEN!**
FOR TODAY, ANYWAY. **THAT** MEANS...
I CAN MAKE **ROYAL DECREES.**

I DECREE THAT TODAY IS "FEED THE QUEEN AN APPLE WHENEVER SHE WANTS ONE" DAY!

YES, MY QUEEN!
AT ONCE, MY QUEEN!
!

IT'S **GOOD** TO BE THE QUEEN!

CARPET, ARE THERE ANY MORE APPLES?

WHOOSH

HEY, WHAT ARE YOU--?

SEE, RAJAH? THIS JOB DOESN'T **HAVE** TO BE BORING!

WHAT ELSE CAN YOU JUGGLE, CARPET?

WOW!

UM, CARPET, I DON'T KNOW IF THAT'S A GOOD IDEA--
WHOMP

WELL, THAT'S WHAT HAPPENS WHEN YOU MESS WITH RAJAH.

HMM, WHAT ELSE COULD I DO FOR ENTERTAINMENT UNTIL MY FATHER FEELS BETTER?

WELL, ASK A SILLY QUESTION...

RAJAH, DON'T TELL ME **YOU** ARE TRYING TO ENTERTAIN ME **TOO!**

WHAM

POK POK
POK POK POK

clap
clap
clap

AND FOR OUR NEXT ACT...
WHAT...

...IS THE **MEANING** OF ALL THIS?
FATHER! YOU'RE **ALL BETTER!**

YES, AND I HOPE I DIDN'T INTERRUPT YOUR LITTLE TALENT SHOW!
WELL, IT'S JUST THAT...

...ALADDIN **WAS** ABOUT TO DO SOME **CARD TRICKS!**
End

SOMETHING TO SING ABOUT

AHHHH...NOPE! AH-AHHH?
SOUNDS LIKE ARIEL IS PRACTICING.

OH AHHH LA-LA-LA...NOPE!
BUT DAT'S NOT ANY SONG I EVER TAUGHT HER.

ARIEL, WHAT IS DAT YOU ARE SINGING?
I'M TRYING TO WRITE A SONG.

DERE IS NO TRY. AND RIGHT NOW, IT LOOKS LIKE "DO NOT."

I WANT TO WRITE SOMETHING THAT PEOPLE CAN ENJOY...

...BUT ALSO SING ALONG TO!

I WANT IT TO SPEAK TO THE HEART! THE SOUL!

WHAT'S IT ABOUT?
I HAVE NO IDEA.

ARIEL, A SONG MUSTN'T COME FROM THE LISTENER. IT HAS TO COME FROM ***YOU.***

TO SPEAK TO THE SOUL, IT HAS TO ***COME*** FROM THE SOUL!

NOW TELL ME, GIRL...WHAT INSPIRES YOUR PASSION FOR LIFE?

I FOUND ONE OF ***THESE!*** ISN'T IT ***NEAT?***
MARVELOUS.

LET'S TAKE A LOOK AT YOUR LYRICS.
"OOOOH YA-YAH, NO-NO, HEY-HEY. LA-LA-LA, YEAH-YEAH, WOO."

THE WOO IS UNDERLINED. LIKE ***"WOO!"***
YES, I SEE DAT.

I WAS WORKING ON THE REFRAIN.

YES, WELL, YOU SHOULD REFRAIN FROM WRITING LYRICS LIKE DESE.

OKAY, I HAVE NEW LYRICS. TELL ME WHAT YOU THINK.

"I LOVE THE OCEAN, BUT I WANT TO TRAVEL. SEE BEYOND WHAT I KNOW, EXPLORE, BUT FATHER DOESN'T AGREE!"

MUCH BETTER! NOW WE JUST HAVE TO WORK ON RHYMING. AND RHYTHM.
WHAT ARE THOSE?

IT'S STRANGE, BECAUSE I KNOW YOU'VE LEARNED WHAT I TAUGHT YOU, BUT SOMEHOW... YOU DIDN'T.

TRY TO COUNT THE SYLLABLES IN EACH PHRASE. IF YOU GET THEM TO THE SAME NUMBER, THE SONG FLOWS BETTER-- THAT'S THE RHYTHM.

IF THE LAST SYLLABLE OF SOME LINES SOUND LIKE THE ONES AT THE ENDS OF OTHER LINES, DAT'S THE RHYME!

IT MAY BE HARD WORK, THE PROCESS IS LONG, BUT DAT IS THE WAY ONE MAKES UP A SONG!

MY LOVE OF THE OCEAN IS DEEP AND TRUE! LA-LA-LA-LA, LA-LA-LA-LA, LA-LA-LA-LA, **WOO!**
AT LEAST IT'S HONEST.

End

INSOMNIA

I DON'T KNOW WHY, BUT I JUST CAN'T GET TO SLEEP.

MAYBE SOME LIGHT READING WILL HELP.

NOW WHAT?

IT'S SUCH A LOVELY NIGHT.

AND THE MOON IS FULL AND BEAUTIFUL!

SIGH IS AN ECLIPSE TOO MUCH TOO ASK?

CAN'T SLEEP, MY DEAR?
UNFORTUNATELY NOT.

IT HAPPENS TO ME ALL THE TIME.

I THINK IT'S BECAUSE I CARRY AROUND TEA ALL DAY. ALL OF THAT CAFFEINE!

HAVE YOU CONSIDERED CHAMOMILE TEA?
THE MASTER LIKES HIS TEA TO HAVE BITE.

I HEARD VOICES. IT SEEMS I'M NOT THE ONLY ONE WHO CAN'T SLEEP.

WE'VE BEEN TRYING TO THINK OF ANYTHING TO HELP.

WE COULD TRY COUNTING SHEEP!

I'M A CLOCK. ALL I DO ALL DAY IS KEEP COUNT.

I OVERHEARD YOU DISCUSSING COUNTING SHEEP. ALLOW ME TO HELP.

I HAVE BEEN AT THE WINDOW ALL NIGHT. THERE ARE NO SHEEP AS FAR AS I COULD SEE.

I LIKE TO KEEP A LIGHT FOR THE MASTER ON THE DARKEST OF NIGHTS.
BUT IT'S A BIG, BRIGHT FULL MOON TONIGHT.

I LIKE TO KEEP IN PRACTICE?

I HEARD EVERYONE TALKING. IS SOMETHING WRONG?
EVERYTHING IS FINE. WE JUST CAN'T SLEEP.

AND BY THE LOOK ON YOUR FACE, WE ALL HAVE TO BE UP SOON ANYWAY.
THE LOOK ON MY FACE IS EXHAUSTION.

SHE IS CORRECT. DAWN APPROACHES, AND WE HAVE OUR CHORES TO START ON.
I JUST HOPE WE HAVE THE ENERGY.

End

GREAT MINDS

I'LL TRADE YOU MY CANTEEN FOR THAT TELESCOPE-HOLDER.

WAIT! I JUST TRADED MY TELESCOPE FOR A CANTEEN HOLDER!

I WANTED TO GET YOU A GIFT.
I GUESS GREAT MINDS **DO** THINK ALIKE.
THEY DO THIS EVERY WEEK.
End

SHADOW PUPPETS

OH CALM DOWN, PASCAL...

...IT'S JUST **ME!**
WHEW!
End

RING IN THE NEW YEAR

THIS IS GOING TO BE THE BEST NEW YEAR'S CELEBRATION THIS TOWN HAS EVER SEEN!

LOOKING GREAT!
HIGHER, LING! I CAN'T REACH!

WHAT YEAR IS IT? DOG? RAT? EMU?
AN EMU?
NOTHING. WHAT'S AN EMU WITH YOU?

ACTUALLY, IT'S THE YEAR OF THE DRAGON.
MY OWN YEAR? OH, WE'VE GOT TO ***CELEBRATE!***

WE NEED TO HAVE FIREWORKS!

NO! A PARADE FLOAT!

I COULD HAVE MY OWN BALLOON!

THIS IS ONLY DAY ONE. LET'S START WITH NAPKINS.

NOBODY WANTS TO BE HONORED WITH BORING NAPKINS.
THE BEST PARTIES ARE MADE IN THE LITTLE DETAILS.

JUST THINK, AT EVERY TABLE WHEN EVERY PERSON SITS TO EAT, THEY WILL SEE THEIR OWN PERSONAL DRAGON!

OH! I GET IT! LIKE ***THIS!***

IF ONLY WE CELEBRATED A YEAR OF THE SWAN!

MAYBE I COULD HOST THE WHOLE EVENT! GIVE A SPEECH ABOUT WHAT DRAGONS MEAN TO EVERYBODY?

WE HAVE ALL OF THAT COVERED ALREADY--HOW OUR CELEBRATIONS WARD OFF THE DRAGON "NIAN" EACH YEAR. JUST ENJOY THE PARTY.
WHY DOES NIAN ALWAYS GET THE ATTENTION?

WELL AT LEAST LET ME DO THE COUNTDOWN FOR THE BALL DROP.
BALL DROP?

YOU MEAN JIE CAI CENG? THE GODS DESCENDING WITH WEALTH AND PROSPERITY?
YOU KNOW, BEING ANACHRONISTIC CAN BE VERY ALIENATING.

HERE YOU GO! HORNS, CLACKERS, TAKE YOUR PICK!

AND REMEMBER NOT TO USE THEM UNTIL THE MOMENT COMES!

DOES EVERYONE HAVE A NOISEMAKER?

I'M READY TO ROLL!

HAPPY NEW YEAR!

OOOOOOH!

THAT WAS BEAUTIFUL.

SO WHEN DO I OPEN MY PRESENTS?
THOSE ARE FOR THE CHILDREN.
End

WORD OF MOUTH

SMELLS GOOD, MAMA ODIE. WHAT ARE YOU MAKING?
AHH, A VERY SPECIAL MAGIC TO BRING MORE CUSTOMERS INTO THAT BUSINESS OF YOURS.

THANK YOU, BUT I WANT TO EARN MY BUSINESS WITH ***MY OWN*** COOKING.

SPEAKING OF WHICH, I NEED TO GET BACK THERE.

WHAT THE GIRL DOESN'T KNOW WILL ONLY HELP HER.

HELLO, AND WELCOME TO TIANA'S PALACE! IT'S ALWAYS NICE TO SEE NEW FACES.

WE WERE...JUST WALKING BY, AND JUST KNEW WE HAD TO EAT HERE.
I HOPE YOU BROUGHT AN APPETITE.

THAT'S JUST IT. WE WERE ON OUR WAY ***FROM LUNCH!***

I EVEN HAVE LEFTOVERS.
I'LL GET THE DESSERT MENU, THEN.

TABLE FOR FOUR?

WE WERE WAND'RING THROUGH THE TOWN, HANKERING FOR SOME LUNCH, WHEN ALL AT ONCE IT STUCK US...AN OVERWHELMING HUNCH!

WE'LL EACH HAVE A GLASS OF WATER, AND SALAD WITH BACON BITS. A MESS OF BUTTERY PO' BOYS, AND A SIDE OF CHEESY GRITS!

RIGHT THIS WAY. FROM HARMONY TO HOMINY.

WHAT DO YOU HAVE THAT'S NOT SEAFOOD?

HUSH PUPPIES! THAT'LL BE DIFFERENT!

BRUSSELS SPROUTS! BROCCOLI! BRUSSELS SPROUTS! BROCCOLI!

I'M TRYING TO BREAK SOME OLD HABITS, SO...
LET ME GUESS... WELL DONE, HEAVY ON THE GARLIC?
YES!

WHAT A BUSY DAY! IS THERE A PARADE OR A FESTIVAL YOU DIDN'T TELL ME ABOUT?

NOT THAT I KNOW ABOUT. MOST OF THESE FOLKS AREN'T REGULARS, SO IF I DIDN'T HEAR ABOUT IT, I DON'T KNOW HOW THEY WOULD'VE.
WHY DON'T WE JUST ASK THEM?

SO WHAT BRINGS YOU IN TODAY? THE FESTIVAL?
RANDOM CRAVING.
I'M NOT FOND OF PARADES.
I'M TIRED OF THE SAME GARBAGE EVERY DAY. TREAT YOURSELF!

TIANA! SIT DOWN! YOU'RE FRAZZLED, AREN'T YOU?
THE RESTAURANT WAS SWAMPED TODAY! I MEAN LITERAL SWAMP CREATURES.

YOU FINISHED THE SPELL, DIDN'T YOU?
YOU NEVER WANT TO LEAVE A SPELL UNFINISHED, IN CASE IT DECIDES TO FINISH ITSELF.

I JUST WANT TO DO THIS MY WAY. I WANT TO EARN MY SUCCESS.
YOU EARNED SOME GOOD FRIENDS. THAT'S SUCCESS.

BESIDES, MY MAGIC GOT THEM IN THE DOOR. YOUR MAGIC GONNA KEEP THEM COMING BACK!
End

ROCK TALK

ALRIGHT BLONDIE, I THINK WE'RE GOOD TO DITCH THIS PLACE AND GET MOVING-- OH. WOULD YOU LOOK AT THAT? I LEFT DIRT ALL OVER YOUR FLOOR.

WOW! THE SURROUNDING AREA HAS A HIGHER CARBON CONCENTRATION THAN I EXPECTED, EVIDENCE OF OXIDIZED IRON, AND OH! LOOK! FELDSPAR!
YOU *DID* SAY YOU'VE NEVER BEEN OUTSIDE, RIGHT?

THERE WASN'T MUCH READING MATERIAL IN THE TOWER. I'VE READ A BOOK ON GEOLOGY ABOUT...7,462 TIMES.

YOU KNOW WHAT BLONDIE? YOU... ROCK.
GROAN
End

MOGNIPICENK

HELLO, BELLE, THE MOST ***MOGNIPICENK*** WOMAN IN TOWN.

MOGNIPICENK?
NO, MAYBE IT'S NAGMIFIOCNT? MOQMIPLEENT? NAGMLPLCOMT?
HMM...
Mognificent

HELLO, BELLE, THE MOST ***GOODEST*** WOMAN IN TOWN.
HANDKERCHIEF FOR YOUR SWEATY PALMS, GASTON?
End

BIRTHDAY WISH

HAPPY BIRTHDAY!

THESE GIFTS ARE FROM ME, OF COURSE.
FATHER, YOU SHOULDN'T HAVE!

YOU DON'T LIKE THEM?

IT'LL TAKE ME UNTIL MY NEXT BIRTHDAY TO FIND OUT.

HERE! I SAW THIS, AND THOUGHT YOU WOULD LOVE IT, SO I PICKED IT UP RIGHT AWAY.

DEFINE "PICKED UP."
I PAID FOR IT, FAIR AND SQUARE!

WELL IT'S ABSOLUTELY PERFECT. THANK YOU.

OH, THANK YOU, TOO, ABU. NOW I HAVE TWO OF THEM.
NO, IT'S THE SAME ONE.

ON THIS MOMENTOUS OCCASION OF TURNING--ACTUALLY, I WON'T ASK, IT'S NEVER POLITE, BUT HOWEVER OLD YOU ARE, SUBTRACT THREE, YOU LOOK GREAT--

--ANYWAY, I HUMBLY GRANT YOU ONE BIRTHDAY WISH. ANYTHING YOUR HEART DESIRES!

THAT'S A THING? MY BIRTHDAY IS NEXT MONTH!

JUST FOR HER. I'M STILL NOT SURE YOU HAVE A HEART. JUST DESIRES.

SO WHAT'LL IT BE? A PONY? AN ARMY? A PONY ARMY? WOULDN'T THAT LOOK CUTE MARCHING INTO WAR... NOT REALLY YOUR STYLE.

HOW ABOUT A NON-MAGIC LAMP? IT GRANTS THE WISH OF LIGHT, AND THAT'S ABOUT IT. AND A YEAR'S SUPPLY OF LAMP OIL!

THANK YOU, BUT I ALREADY HAVE PLENTY IN MY LIFE TO KEEP ME HAPPIER THAN I'D EVER DREAMED.

DON'T LOOK A WISH HORSE IN THE MOUTH.

EVERYONE HAS ALREADY BEEN SO GENEROUS AND THOUGHTFUL WITH THEIR GIFTS.

WELL, EXCEPT ABU.

A GIFT SHOULD BE SOMETHING FROM THE HEART, FROM ONE PERSON TO ANOTHER. AND I'VE TRIED TO EARN AND DESERVE ALL OF THE THINGS THAT MAKE MY LIFE GREAT, INSTEAD OF JUST WISHING FOR THEM.

YOU UNDERSTAND, RIGHT?
HOW ABOUT THIS? I'D SAY YOU EARNED IT.
I survived the Cave of Wonders and all I got was this shirt.

I DIDN'T KNOW WHAT TO GET YOU. I NEVER DO. PEOPLE TELL ***ME***. IT'S SORT OF MY WHOLE THING.

I'M SORRY. I DO APPRECIATE IT. HOW'S THIS--I WISH WE COULD ALL HAVE A NICE QUIET DINNER TOGETHER.
DONE!

THIS IS AMAZING! YOU'RE USING THE BREAD AS A BOWL!
MY WISH IS TO NOT HAVE TO DO THE DISHES.
End

GLEAM AND GROW

HAPPY BIRTHDAY PASCAL! WHAT SHOULD WE DO FIRST, OPEN YOUR PRESENT OR--OH, OKAY, WE CAN MEASURE YOU.

YOU'VE UM, YOU'VE GROWN ABOUT A QUARTER OF AN INCH!

OH, IT'S NOT SO BAD, WE CAN'T ALL EXPECT TO GROW FOUR FEET A YEAR!
End

WET BOOTS

AURORA, BE A DEAR AND HELP ME CHANGE THESE WET BOOTS.

YOUR BOOTS WOULDN'T BE WET IF YOU HADN'T CHASED THOSE CHILDREN INTO THE POND.

NOW, WHAT KIND OF FAIRY WOULD I BE IF I GAVE UP DURING A GAME OF TAG?

A DRY ONE.
End

ANTSY GODMOTHER

WHAT A LOVELY CASTLE.

WHAT A LOVELY GARDEN.

EVERYTHING IS SO *LOVELY!*

I'M BIBBIDI-BOBBIDI-*BORED!*

I SAW THE MOST MAGNIFICENT DEER YESTERDAY IN THE COURTYARD.

AH, YES, THEY DO GET BOLD THIS TIME OF YEAR!

OH MY! SOMETHING IS DIFFERENT WITH THIS TEA! I FEEL SUDDENLY BOTH RELAXED AND ENERGIZED!

THAT'S NOT THE ONLY RECIPE THAT HAS CHANGED.

I WONDER IF THAT DEER HAS COME BACK.

THERE'S A WINDOW THAT OVERLOOKS THE COURTYARD IN THE EAST WING. LET'S GO SEE!

I DON'T SEE HIM, BUT THE COURTYARD IS SO LARGE.

AH, THAT'S MUCH BETTER!
???

I DON'T SEE ANY DEER, BUT IT'S HARD TO TELL FROM HERE.

PERHAPS THESE WILL HELP.

THANK YOU.

PLEASE TELL ME YOU'RE NOTICING THIS!
I'VE BEEN TRYING NOT TO ENCOURAGE IT.

"I SEE SOME DEER, BUT NOT THE ONE I SAW BEFORE.

"NOW WAIT JUST A MINUTE."

OH MY, THIS IS GETTING OUT OF HAND!

"OR OUT OF **WAND,** I SHOULD SAY!"

THERE'S REALLY NO NEED TO KEEP IMPROVING EVERYTHING.

I KNOW, IT'S JUST THAT I'M HERE TO MAKE EVERYTHING SO MAGICAL FOR YOU, BUT IT ALREADY IS!

AND THAT'S ALL THANKS TO YOU, BUT NOW MY LIFE IS PERFECT. YOU CAN RELAX, AND MAYBE TREAT YOURSELF TO A LITTLE MAGIC.
HMMM...

End

OFF TO WORK

YOU KNOW, GRUMPY, I'VE NEVER ACTUALLY SEEN YOUR WORKPLACE.

THE MINE? NOT MUCH TO SEE. IT'S DARK AND DIRTY AND SMELLY.

LIKE DOPEY'S FEET WHEN HE FORGETS TO WASH 'EM.

WELL THEN, TODAY I'M GOING TO COME SEE THE MINE.

ALL IN FAVOR?
AYE!

AS USUAL, SLEEPY ABSTAINS.

HEIGH-HO. HEIGH-HO. IT'S OFF TO WORK WE GO!

WHAT FUN! DO YOU ALWAYS SING LIKE THIS ON YOUR WAY TO WORK?

WE SURE DO!

BUT WE USUALLY DON'T HAVE AN ARMY OF BEASTS TRAMPING ALONG BEHIND.

MY, IT CERTAINLY IS DARK IN THERE.

IT WAS DOPEY'S TURN TO BRING THE LANTERN.

AAH-AAAHH-AAAAAHHH.

THANKS FOR WAKING UP EARLY TO HELP US OUT, FRIENDS.
JUST THINK HOW MUCH WE COULD BE SAVING ON LANTERN FUEL EVERY YEAR!

GOLLY, THIS FIREFLY LIGHT SURE IS PRETTY!

AAAHHHHH...

...CHOOO!

MAYBE ONE OF US COULD RUN HOME TO GET A LANTERN?

THESE ARE HEAVY. IT TOOK ME YEARS TO GET STRONG ENOUGH TO USE ONE.

THEY ARE AWFULLY HEAVY.

"I GUESS CLEANING UP GETS ME MORE EXERCISE THAN I THOUGHT."
SNEEZY

MINING IS THIRSTY WORK, BUT IT MUST ALL BE WORTH IT WHEN YOU FIND A JEWEL.

PFFT JEWELS ARE FINE, I GUESS.

I JUST LIKE HAVING SOMETHING I'M ALLOWED TO TAKE OUT MY FRUSTRATIONS ON.

OH!

LOOK! I ALREADY FOUND A DIAMOND!

GREAT. TOSS IT OVER THERE WITH THE OTHERS.

THAT'S A PRETTY ONE!
THANK YOU, HAPPY.

BUT IN THE TIME IT TOOK ME TO FIND JUST ONE DIAMOND, YOU EACH MINED DOZENS.

IT TOOK ME MONTHS TO FIND ONE THIS PRETTY WHEN I FIRST STARTED, AND YOU DID IT ON YOUR FIRST DAY.

I GUESS YOU COULD CALL IT A "MINER" MIRACLE?

GREAT WORK TODAY, SNOW!

NOW I KNOW WHY YOU ALL COME HOME SO DIRTY.

THANKS FOR BRUSHING THE DUST AWAY, FRIENDS!

UGH! AS IF TAKING A REGULAR BATH WEREN'T BAD ENOUGH!
End

BATHTIME

IAGO, HAVE YOU SEEN CARPET?

HE NEEDS WASHING, AND YOU KNOW HOW HE HATES THAT.
HAVEN'T SEE HIM.

IF YOU DO, LET US KNOW.
YEAH, MAYBE. I HAVE THINGS TO DO, TOO, YOU KNOW.

YOU CAN COME OUT NOW, RUG-RAT!
End

WORD OF THE DAY

GUESS WHAT TIME IT IS, PASCAL? THAT'S RIGHT, IT'S **WORD OF THE DAY** TIME.
BOTANY

AND TODAY'S WORD IS... ***CONCOLOROUS:*** UNIFORMLY COLORED, OR COLORED THE SAME THROUGHOUT...
BOTANY

CON-*COLOR*-OUS! ***GREAT*** WORD. SO LYRICAL! THE CHALLENGE IS TO FIND A WAY TO USE THE WORD TODAY.

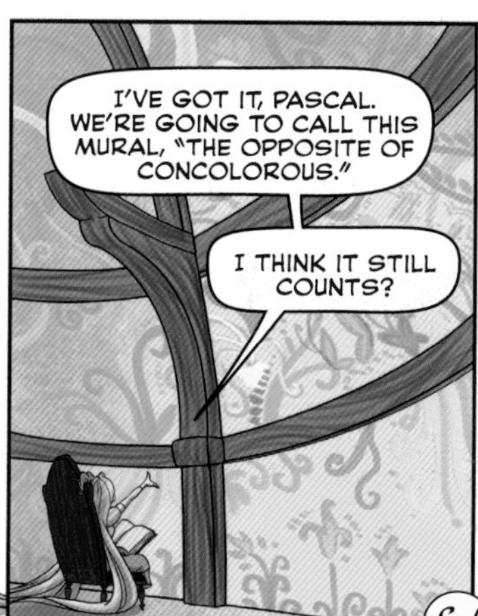
I'VE GOT IT, PASCAL. WE'RE GOING TO CALL THIS MURAL, "THE OPPOSITE OF CONCOLOROUS."
I THINK IT STILL COUNTS?
End

ARCHERY ASSIST

SO, MY WEE APPLE. HOW DO WE TURN YOU INTO APPLE *SLICES,* HERE IN THE *FOREST* WITHOUT ANY *KNIVES?*
HMM...

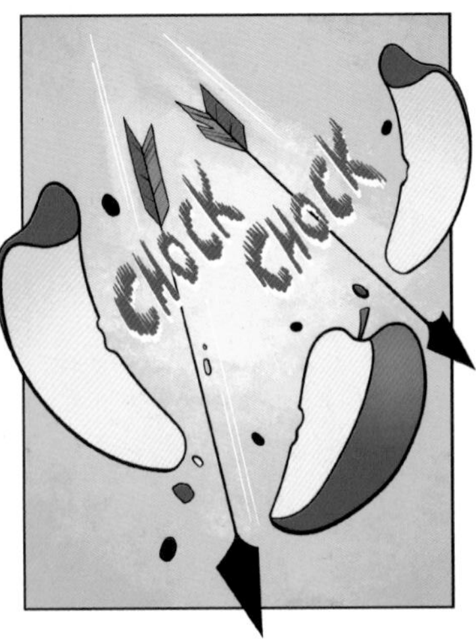
CHOCK
CHOCK

APPLE *SLICES?* BUT *HOW?* THERE AREN'T ANY *KNIVES* OUT HERE.
I IMPROVISED.

HMM...I WANT TO LEAVE A *NOTE* FOR DAD. BUT HOW CAN I MAKE SURE HE *NOTICES* IT?

IDEA

GLORP
GLUP
GLOP

BE
Back
Soon

HMM...

AND SO...
CAN YE DO IT LIKE I'VE DESCRIBED?
OCH, OF COURSE.

THWIP
THWIP
THWIP
THWIP
THWIP

MERIDA, YOUR **ARCHERY** SKILLS MAKE ME **QUIVER!**
OH FATHER, YOUR WORDPLAY IS RIGHT ON **TARGET!**
I LOVE YOU ELINOR

HAPPY ANNIVERSARY, ELINOR!
HOW **ROMANTIC,** FERGUS!

YOU REALLY **CAN** DO ANYTHING WITH YOUR ARROWS, CAN'T YOU?
WHAT DID YOU HAVE IN MIND?

HERE. IS **THIS** THE SPOT?

THWIP
THWIP
THWIP
THWIP

WELL, BOYS? DO YOU LIKE IT?
THWIP
THWIP
THWIP

I'LL TAKE THAT AS A "YES."

OKAY, WEE ONES. LIGHTS OUT!
BOING
BABOING

LET ME GIVE YOU A HAND, MAUDIE!

SFOOK

SEE? LIKE I SAID, "LIGHTS OUT!"

OCH! T RE YOU ARE, M DA! I'M HOPIN OU CAN HELP ME WITH--

--MERIDA? SOMETHING WRONG?

OH DEAR.
Z Z Z Z Z

MERIDA LOVES HELPING US WITH HER ARCHERY SKILLS, BUT WE'VE BEEN RELYING ON HER SKILLS SO OFTEN...
...SHE HASN'T HAD TIME TO ***SLEEP***
AYE, BUT HOW CAN WE MAKE THINGS RIGHT?
LEAVE THAT TO ME.

MERIDA!!!

BEHOLD! A HAMMOCK WORTHY OF SOMEONE WITH YOUR PARTICULAR GIFTS!

I WONDER IF SHE LIKES IT.
I THINK IT'S SAFE TO ASSUME SHE ***DOES***.
End

OAK ISLAND

OOH! A CAVE!

YOU NEVER CAN GUESS WHAT YOU'LL FIND, ONLY THAT IT'S GOING TO BE SOMETHING SPECIAL!

MAYBE SOMETHING NEW, OR SOMETHING OLD AND LOST...

...OR MAYBE A DEAD END.

I THINK I HEAR SOMETHING!

I JUST HAVE TO KNOW WHAT'S ON THE OTHER SIDE!

YIPES!

CAP'N! THE HOLE IS FLOODING!
THE ISLAND IS SINKING!

WE NEED TO STOP THE FLOODING OR WE'LL LOSE THE TREASURE!

WE CAN LAY DOWN SOME PLANKS TO HOLD IT BACK!

THERE! THAT SHOULD DO IT.

I'M SORRY ABOUT FLOODING YOUR TREASURE.
GAH!

DID YOU SEE THAT?
METHINKS IT WAS A MERMAID!
AND SHE SAW OUR STOLEN TREASURE!

FILL IT WITH SAND AND LAY DOWN MORE PLANKS! WE CAN T HER WITH THAT TREASURE!

THEN WE CAN PROTECT THE REST OF THE GOLD THAT WE'RE BURYING OVER THERE!

HELLO!
AHH! CAP'N!

IT'S CLEAR THE MERMAID IS TAUNTING US, MEN. OAK ISLAND IS *CURSED!*

BEST WE LEAVE NOW. WE CAN RETURN FOR OUR TREASURE ANOTHER DAY.

IT SOUNDS LIKE THEY'RE JUST LEAVING ALL THIS BEHIND.

MAYBE THEIR TREASURE IS *CURSED!*

THAT'S SILLY. THESE ARE JUST *THINGS,* AND NOW THEY CAN'T GET TO THEM. THIS IS MY FAULT.

I KNOW HOW I CAN HELP! BUT IT'LL REQUIRE A LOT OF DIGGING!

LUCKILY, WE KNOW WHERE EVERYTHING IS BURIED.
THREE SEPARATE BATCHES OF TREASURE, SO EVEN IF SOMEONE FINDS ONE, THEY'LL NEVER FIND IT *ALL!*

THANK GOODNESS FOR THESE TUNNELS! THERE! ALL IN ONE BIG, NEW PLACE!
End

STORMY NIGHT

WELL...AT LEAST IT'S NOT *THUNDERING!*

CRASH
AAAWWWK!
IAGO?! WHAT'S WRONG?
ROOOOAR
OH, *ABU!* I DIDN'T KNOW YOU WERE SCARED OF THUNDER LIKE IAGO!
I'M NOT SCARED. I JUST WANTED TO... *ERM...PROTECT* YA!

NO, RAJAH. DON'T EVEN *THINK* ABOUT IT!

COME ON, I KNOW YOU ARE THE *BRAVEST* TIGER IN AGRABAH!
YEAH, AND THIS PLACE IS TAKEN!

KRAK-

DON'T WORRY, ALADDIN! EVERYTHING IS *UNDER CONTROL...*
I CAN'T BREATHE!
End

MYSTERIOUS TRAVELS

WHY DO BELLE AND THE MASTER EAT *BEANS* FOR BREAKFAST?
BECAUSE THEY ARE GOOD, CHIP!

AND THEY ARE ALSO PART OF A POPULAR BREAKFAST IN *LONDON!*
OH, I HAVE ALWAYS WANTED TO VISIT LONDON! MAY WE GO TODAY, MY DEAR?

OF COURSE! AND WE'LL LEARN EVERYTHING ABOUT A FULL ENGLISH BREAKFAST.
PHEW, I'M LUCKY TEACUPS DON'T *EAT!*

BONJOUR, MADEMOISELLE! WHERE ARE YOU HEADING?
I'M OFF TO INDIA, LUMIÈRE. DO YOU WANT TO JOIN ME?

THAT WOULD BE *FANTASTIQUE!*

GOOD! YOU CAN BRING FEATHER DUSTER, TOO!
OH, *MERCI!* I'LL GO TELL HER IMMEDIATELY!

WE'LL *DANCE* ALL THE WAY TO INDIA, *MON AMOUR!*
I'D RATHER BE CARRIED IN A COMFORTABLE BAG, *MON CHERI!*

GOOD MORNING, COGSWORTH. HAVE YOU EVER BEEN TO VENICE?
ERM, NO, MADEMOISELLE.

WHAT ABOUT TRAVELING THERE WITH ME LATER TODAY?
PARBLEU! I'D BE DELIGHTED TO!

OH, YES, YOU ARE INVITED TOO!
WOOF WOOF

SO BELLE IS TAKING US TO INDIA.
NO, WE'RE GOING TO LONDON FIRST!

I DIDN'T KNOW YOU AND THE OBJECTS WERE PLANNING TRIPS ALL OVER THE WORLD...
YOU CAN COME, TOO! WE ARE JUST ABOUT TO LEAVE...

EACH OF THESE BOOKS IS SET IN A DIFFERENT PLACE. WE'LL VISIT THEM ALL IN ONE SINGLE DAY!

SO THAT'S WHAT YOU MEAN BY "READING IS LIKE TRAVELING"! NOW I GET IT!
BUT...DON'T YOU THINK YOU ARE ALL GETTING CARRIED AWAY?
THE PARASOL IS FOR INDIA, THE UMBRELLA IS FOR LONDON, AND THE PILLOW IS FOR EVERYWHERE...
End

HOMEWORK

ARIEL, I SEE YOU ARE KEEPING UP ON YOUR HOMEWORK?

I AM! LOOK! I'M MAKING A MAP!

AND YOU EXPLORED THE AREAS I ASSIGNED?
OF COURSE! WHY?

BECAUSE "HERE THERE BE" NO MONSTERS ***I'VE*** EVER SEEN.

I THOUGHT SOME MONSTERS WOULD MAKE THE MAP INTRIGUING!

THE POINT OF THESE ASSIGNMENTS IS TO EDUCATE YOU, FILL YOUR HEAD WITH WHAT YOU'LL NEED TO GET BY IN LIFE.

BUT WHAT IF WHAT I NEED IN LIFE IS ADVENTURE?

YOU DON'T SEE MY PROBLEM AS A PROBLEM, DO YOU?

THERE WAS SO LITTLE OUT THERE TO LOOK AT. I HAD TO DRAW SOMETHING!

THERE WAS NOTHING BUT ROCKS AND CORAL AND MORE ROCKS.

THOSE BORING DETAILS ARE MARKERS SO PEOPLE DON'T GET LOST.

HOW CAN ANYONE DISCOVER SOMETHING NEW IF THEY DON'T GET LOST LOOKING?
BY BORROWING SOMEONE ELSE'S MAP.

MAYBE CARTOGRAPHY ISN'T YOUR STRONG SUIT. DID YOU DISCOVER ANY PLANT LIFE?

I DID! I SAW SOMETHING LIKE SEAWEED, BUT BLUISH PURPLE! AND IT WAS THICK!

IT WAS DRIFTING UP, THEN WAVING AROUND...
AND WHAT IS IT CALLED?

I DON'T KNOW, SO I NAMED IT "TWILIGHT DANCEGRASS"!
IT'S CALLED LAVER.

DID YOU SEE ANY INTERESTING ANIMALS WHILE YOU WERE OUT?

A STAR DRAGON! IT LOOKED LIKE A COLOSSAL SEA HORSE WITH STARFISH SKIN!

AND IT WAS HUGE! WHEN IT SWUNG ITS TAIL, THE *TIDES CHANGED!*

DID YOU REALLY SEE THAT?
NO, JUST A WHALE LOOKING FOR EXOTIC PLANKTON.

I WAS HOPING YOU WOULD FIND SOMETHING THAT INSPIRED YOU TO LEARN. YOU'RE SMART, BUT RARELY APPLY YOURSELF TO YOUR EDUCATION.

AT LEAST TOMORROW I KNOW YOU'LL GIVE YOUR ALL FOR SEBASTIAN'S MUSIC CLASS.

OH! WE'RE LEARNING A NEW SONG ABOUT AN OCTOPUS! HIS EIGHT ARMS LINE UP WITH THE EIGHT NOTES IN THE SCALE!

I HAVE TO READ UP ON THEM SO I CAN DO THE PIECE JUSTICE.
SO YOU--
SHH! PLEASE! LEARNING!
End

BRAG RACE

FACE IT, LI SHANG, YOU MAY BE BIG AND STRONG BUT *RACING* IS WHAT MULAN DOES *BEST!*

THAT'S CLEARLY JUST NOT TRUE.
WHA...? KHAN, YOU'RE *MY* HORSE!

YOU...YOU... HORSE TRAITOR!

BUT GLOATING IS WHAT *I* DO BEST.
THAT'S WHAT YOU GET FOR GLOATING, MUSHU.
End

AN APPLE A DAY

VERY WELL, MEEKO.

I THINK YOU'VE BURNED OFF ENOUGH ENERGY TO HAVE THAT SNACK NOW.
End

STREET ART

LOVELY DAY, ISN'T IT?
IT IS, PRINCESS, BUT I HEAR THEY'RE CALLING FOR RAIN LATER.

WELL, IT'S NOT RAINING YET! WE CAN EITHER SIT AROUND AND WAIT, OR ENJOY THE SUNSHINE!

WHAT ARE YOU DOING, PRINCESS?
DECORATING THE TOWN SQUARE.

YOU MIGHT NEED MORE CHALK.

WHY ARE THE ANTS ALL DIFFERENT COLORS?
WHAT ANTS?

THOSE ANTS.

OH, THOSE AREN'T ANTS. IT WILL ALL MAKE SENSE SOON. GOOD THINGS COME TO THOSE WHO WAIT!
WHAT IF I DON'T WANT TO WAIT?

PATIENCE IS A VIRTUE. TRUST ME ON--WHERE'D SHE GO?
THERE WAS A BUTTERFLY.

EXCUSE ME, PRINCESS, THOSE STARS ARE YELLOW.
THOSE AREN'T STARS.

THOSE STARS ARE BLUE.
THOSE AREN'T STARS, EITHER.

AT NIGHT THEY ALL MATCH. THESE DON'T MATCH.
THANK YOU FOR NOTICING.

YOU SHOULD GET THE SAME COLOR CHALK. IS THAT ORION?
≈SIGH≈ HOW DID YOU GUESS?

YOU MIGHT WANT TO GET INSIDE, AND TRY AGAIN TOMORROW, PRINCESS.

I'VE SPENT TOO MANY DAYS WAITING FOR TOMORROW.

EVERYONE! FOLLOW ME!

THIS INN HAS A COVERED BALCONY!

SOMETIMES YOU CAN SIT AROUND AND WAIT, AND MAKE THE MOST OF THE DAY.
End

MORNING SWIM

I'M HEADING TO THE BEACH, ERIC. BACK IN A BIT!
SHE NEVER MISSES HER MORNING SWIM.
YOU COULD LEARN SOMETHING FROM HER, SIRE. EXERCISE IS IMPORTANT!

THE BEST PART OF MY MORNING IS GETTING TO SEE THE TWO OF YOU!

AND IT'S ABSOLUTELY WORTH THE MANY LEAGUES WE HAVE TO SWIM TO REACH YOU.

DON'T WORRY ABOUT HIM--SEBASTIAN'S IN THE BEST SHAPE HE'S EVEN BEEN.
I CAN PLAY THE CONGA UNTIL THE DANCERS ARE THE ONES BEGGING FOR A BREAK!
End

LUNGE/CRUNCH

HELLO, TIANA!
SSHHH! KEEP IT DOWN.

LOUIS IS IN THE MIDDLE OF EXERCISING AND I DON'T WANT TO DISTURB HIM.

HOW IS THAT EXERCISING?
HE SAYS IT'S A CROSS BETWEEN A LUNGE AND A CRUNCH.

SO... "LUNCH"?
End

AHOY MATEYS

THAR SHE BLOWS, PASCAL!
THE WIND, SHE BE FIERCE! I'M NOT SURE IF WE'RE GOING TO MAKE IT!

AVAST YE SCURVY DOGS! STOP YER HORNSWAGGLIN' AND KEEP A WEATHER EYE OPEN! WE'RE NO LANDLUBBERS!

NOTHING BEATS THE DOLDRUMS LIKE A DAY AT SEA.
End

CORN-ERED

munch
munch

zZZZIP

MEEKO!
End

BRAIN TEASER

WHAT'S YOUR FATHER UP TO, PRINCESS?

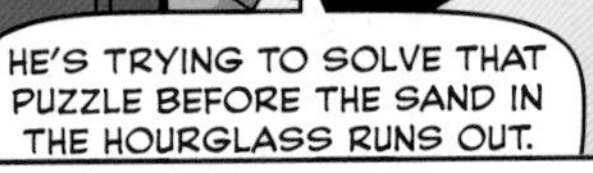
HE'S TRYING TO SOLVE THAT PUZZLE BEFORE THE SAND IN THE HOURGLASS RUNS OUT.

HAVE YOU CONSIDERED GETTING HIM A BIGGER HOURGLASS?
End

TREE TALK

GRANDMOTHER WILLOW, DO YOU EVER GET LONELY OUT HERE WITH NO ONE TO TALK TO?

GOODNESS NO, MY DEAR! DON'T YOU KNOW TREES ARE THE BIGGEST GOSSIPS THERE ARE?
REALLY?

OF COURSE! THE WIND IS ALWAYS ***WHISPERING*** THROUGH THEM!

SO, YOU'RE TELLING ME THAT TREES LOVE TO GOSSIP?
YOU SHOULD HEAR ALL THE CHATTER!

ASH IS VERY NERVOUS, ALWAYS TREMBLING... ***SYCAMORE*** IS NEVER FEELING WELL...

...AND ***OAK*** IS A BIT NUTTY, BUT ***DOGWOOD*** ISN'T NEARLY SO BAD AS THEY SAY.

...ITS ***BARK*** IS WORSE THAN ITS BITE!

NOW, ALL JOKING ASIDE, GOSSIP CAN BE HURTFUL!

WHY, THOSE POOR EVERGREENS ARE ALWAYS LEFT OUT.
OH, NO!

OH, YES, THEY'RE REALLY PINING TO BE PART OF THE POPLAR CROWD!

AND WHY DO YOU THINK WE WILLOWS ARE ALWAYS WEEPING!
GROAN

I HAD NO IDEA THAT TREES WERE SO TEMPERAMENTAL! BUT WE REALLY SHOULD BE GOING...

OH, WELL, DO BE CAREFUL WHAT YOU SAY ON YOUR WAY BACK TO THE VILLAGE!

THAT CORNFIELD IS FULL OF EARS! AND DON'T TRUST THE POTATOES!

THEY'VE GOT EYES EVERYWHERE!
GROAN
End

BEASTLY

I TELL YOU, LUMIERE, THAT BLASTED MONGREL HAS GOTTEN ON MY LAST NERVE!
IT TRACKS MUD ACROSS THE CARPETS, CHASES THE THROW PILLOWS...

AH, OUI, MON AMI! BUT AT LEAST YOU ARE ARE NOT ZE PREFERRED CHEW TOY!

EXACTLY! IT'S TIME SOMETHING WAS DONE ABOUT THAT UNRULY BEAST!
WHO, ME?

ROWF ROWF ROWF!

AAAAA!

SNARRRL!

I'M SURE THERE'S A GREAT STORY THERE...
End

STRENGTH IN NUMBERS

YOU WANT TO TRY IT?

UNNPH...

DON'T FEEL BAD, YOU'VE NEVER HAD ACCESS TO THE ROYAL FAMILY'S SECRET TRAINING METHOD.

OOOF A BIT MORE OF THIS AND I'LL BE READY TO WIELD THE CLAN SWORD.
End

EUGENE, LET DOWN YOUR HAIR

RAPUNZEL, I'VE DECIDED IT'S TIME TO GET MY HAIR CUT.

I THOUGHT YOU SAID THAT YOU GOT IT CUT TWO WEEKS AGO?

HAVEN'T YOU NOTICED? IT'S GROWN BY A FRACTION OF A FRACTION OF AN INCH.

I NEVER MEASURED THAT CLOSELY.

USUALLY I'D BE NERVOUS SEEING A NEW BARBER.

BUT I'M NOT WORRIED, THE PALACE MUST HAVE AN AMAZING BARBERSHOP. AND THE MOST TALENTED BARBERS IN ALL THE LAND.

ACTUALLY, THE PALACE BARBER CALLED IN SICK TODAY.
HIC!

OKAY, NOW I'M NERVOUS.

SO WHAT'LL IT BE? SHAVE AND SHAMPOO? THE WHOLE SPA TREATMENT?
JUST A HAIRCUT, PLEASE.

YOU HAVE CUT HAIR BEFORE, RIGHT?

OH, SURE. HORSE HAIR. DOG HAIR. GOAT HAIR...

ANY HUMAN HAIR?
DEFINE HUMAN.

WHAT WE NEED IS A GUINEA PIG.

OH, I'VE DONE PIGS, TOO. BIG PIGS **AND** SMALL PIGS.

DO PIGS EVEN HAVE THAT MUCH HAIR?

NOT WHEN I WAS DONE WITH THEM, THEY DIDN'T!

I THINK WE NEED TO FIND SOMEONE TO TEST YOUR BARBER SKILLS ON.

PERHAPS SOMEONE WITH FREE TIME ON HIS HANDS.

JUST A LITTLE OFF THE TOP.

LATER...
I'M PROUD OF YOU. AND YOUR HAIR LOOKS GREAT.

SHORTY DID A GREAT JOB. I CAN'T BELIEVE HOW NERVOUS I WAS. THANK GOODNESS YOU'RE SO BRAVE, YOU DIDN'T SEEM WORRIED AT ALL.

NO, NOT WORRIED AT ALL.
End

SCALE MODEL

GUARDS! GUARDS!
KNOCK
KNOCK

I GUESS I'LL HAVE TO LET US IN.
DO YOU REALLY MEAN TO SCALE THAT ENTIRE WALL?

INCREDIBLE!

HOW DID YOU GET SUCH AN AMAZING GRIP?
ALL THAT HEARTH SCRUBBING!
End

COUNTING STARS

I COUNT ONE THOUSAND, SIX HUNDRED AND TWENTY-TWO. I THINK THAT'S TWO MORE THAN YESTERDAY!
End

THE END

THE VILLAGERS CHEERED AS THEIR CARRIAGE RODE INTO THE SUNSET. ***THE END.***
AND THEN WHAT HAPPENED?

THEY LIVED HAPPILY EVER AFTER.
AND THEN WHAT HAPPENED?

THEY HAVE ANOTHER EXCITING ADVENTURE, WHICH I'LL TELL YOU ABOUT TOMORROW NIGHT.
AND ***THEN*** WHAT HAPPENED?

WHAT HAPPENED NEXT WAS...YOU WENT TO BED!
AWW.
End